Benjamin Pugh, George Baker

Observations on the Climates of Naples, Rome, Nice

in a letter to Sir George Baker, Bart. M.D. - in which is inserted some

advice to those who intend visiting those places in pursuit of health

Benjamin Pugh, George Baker

Observations on the Climates of Naples, Rome, Nice
in a letter to Sir George Baker, Bart. M.D. - in which is inserted some advice to those who intend visiting those places in pursuit of health

ISBN/EAN: 9783337382278

Printed in Europe, USA, Canada, Australia, Japan

Cover: Foto ©Andreas Hilbeck / pixelio.de

More available books at **www.hansebooks.com**

OBSERVATIONS

ON THE

CLIMATES

OF

NAPLES, ROME, NICE, &c.

In a LETTER to

Sir GEORGE BAKER, Bart. M.D.

In which is inferted

Some ADVICE to thofe who intend vifiting thofe PLACES
in Purfuit of HEALTH.

By BENJAMIN PUGH, M.D.

——————Si quid novifti rectius iftis,
Candidus imperti ; fi non, his utere mecum.
HOR. Epift.

LONDON,
Printed for G. ROBINSON, No. 25, Pater-nofter-Row.
MDCCLXXXIV.

━━━━━━━━━━━━━━━━━━━━━━
━━━━━━━━━━━━━━━━━━━━━━

T O

Sir George Baker, Bart. M. D,

Montpellier, April 30, 1784.

SIR,

AS three years are nearly elapſed ſince you entruſted to my care your very worthy and reſpeçtable patient Mr. Wollaſton, *at that time* labouring under a very ſevere and obſtinate diſ-

B   order;

order; I think it my duty to explain to you in what manner I have acquitted myfelf of the charge. To make you a partaker of the joy which fo fenfibly affects me on this occafion, it might be enough to communicate to you the *bare* information of this gentleman's recovery; but I think myfelf called upon to go. farther; I feel an obligation to give you a particular account of the fucceffive fteps which have been employed to bring about that happy event. I fhall take the liberty alfo occafionally to infert the obfervations which occurred to me on my travels, relative to thofe difeafes which prevail moft in each country, and the influence which each climate might *poffibly* have in aggravating, if not in producing them.

4   It

It has been the fashion of our countrymen, afflicted with pulmonary diforders, to feek health under the milder
fun of Nice or Naples; but far the
greater part of fuch patients have, I
believe, either returned difappointed in
their purfuits, or fallen victims to this
fatal error. In fuch cafes, I give the
preference to the air of Provence or
Languedoc, in the South of France;
and am fupported in this idea by reafons
which fhall be hereafter given. But as
I fhall only mention *facts and things*, my
intention is not to enter into any literary
difpute with any one, as I am convinced
that the moft ingenious man on earth
cannot form or devife a fentence, but
the wit of another can find fomething in
it whereat to carp and cavil. My view

in

in this publication is to render fervice to thofe of my countrymen, whofe infirm ftate of health may force them to feek relief in foreign climes; and if any one receives the fmalleft benefit from the following fheets, the happinefs of the writer will be perfectly complete.

You may remember we left England in the beginning of July, in the year 1781. We paffed by way of Oftend to the German Spa, where Mr. Wollafton, for the fpace of one month, drank the waters of the Pohun and Geronftere fountains, ufed the warm baths twice in the week, and continued his medicines; not omitting to take exercife on horfeback every morning. Thefe waters, &c. agreed fo well with him, that by the end of the month

month the œdematous fwellings in his
legs were quite gone; the ulcer, which
was in one of them; quite healed ; and
his fpirits fo well recovered, that he found
himfelf perfectly able to proceed on his
journey for Italy. At Aix-la-Chapelle,
where we ftaid ten days, he made the
fame ufe of the waters and baths as at
the Spa, and found them of no lefs
benefit. I omit to mention to you the
name of each town through which we
paffed, as it would be but an uninterefting
detail. It fuffices to fay, that by the
route of Germany and Switzerland we
entered Italy, and made the beft of our
way to Naples, where we arrived in the
month of November. Here we took up
our refidence until April, 1782. This
winter proved the moft fevere that was

ever

ever remembered by the oldeft perfon living in this city. Three nights fharp froft in the month of January killed all the orange, lemon, pomegranate, and other tender trees in the environs, and caufed more damage than can be repaired by a long fucceffion of the mildeft winters. Shortly after our arrival I was feized with violent inflammations in my eyes, and an intenfe head-ach, with rheumatic pains in various parts of my body; complaints to which I had ever before been a perfect ftranger. My wife complained of head-aches, but not in fo violent a degree; Mrs. Wollafton was affected much in the fame manner, and Mr. Wollafton received very little, *if any*, benefit by his ftay there. As this climate had been fo long celebrated for

its

its mildnefs, I was furprifed at the obfti-
nate continuance of the complaints of our
own family, and likewife at the numbers
of difeafed and miferable objects I met in
every part of the city. I refolved to
vifit the public hofpitals, where I beheld
mifery in the extreme; fevers of *every*
clafs, but *fcarce one* where the lungs had
not been primarily concerned; rheumatifms, dropfies, fcrophulas, confumptions,
ulcers of every kind, and venereal difeafes without number.

To affign a caufe for the chief of thefe
effects, I began to reafon thus with
myfelf—The fea in the Bay of Naples
has no tides, or indeed next to none,
as it has never more than fix inches;
its furface is generally as placid as a

fifhfiſh-pond, and the mountains and high lands, which ſurround the bay, prevent a free circulation of air, ſo that the atmoſphere muſt be almoſt always loaded with ſaline, marine particles—the ſudden tranſitions from the exceſs of heat to that of cold within the ſpace of the ſame day—but, above all, the wind called *lo Scirocco,* which ſo frequently blows in this country, and whoſe effects are ſcarcely conceivable by thoſe who have not experienced them.—All theſe things taken together, cannot but render this climate extremely dangerous to tender and unreſiſting conſtitutions ; and to ſome or all of theſe cauſes do I attribute that unbalmy quality of the air of Naples, ſo peculiarly unfavourable to conſumptive lungs.

During

During my refidence in this town there arrived a moft amiable young Englifh nobleman, whofe lungs were difeafed. He came with a defign to fpend fome of the winter months; but the air had fuch an effect upon him, that he could fcarce breathe : fo that in eight or nine days he was obliged to leave it, and precipitately bend his courfe to the South of France. Examples alfo are not wanting of others who, difcovering their error when it was too late, and attempting to remove when nature was too much exhaufted, were arrefted by death in their flight.

On the laft day of April, the weather beginning to grow too warm, we left Naples, and went to Rome, where we made

C

fome

some stay, as the air perfectly agreed with Mr. Wollaston. With respect to myself, in eight or nine days time, the head-ach and inflammation in the eyes, which were more or less troublesome to me during my residence at Naples, entirely took their leave. I heard from the best authority, that an English gentleman, who had been troubled for a considerable time with an asthma, which would never permit him to remain during the winter in London, came regularly from thence to spend that part of the year at Rome, where he always found that relief which he had in vain sought for before at Naples, Nice, and other parts of Italy.

On the second of July following, we left this city to go to the hot baths of Pisa,

Pifa, which are faid to be extremely beneficial in gouty cafes, and difeafes in
the liver. I found thefe waters much of
the fame heat and quality as the King's
bath, at Bath, in Somerfetfhire. About
two miles from the baths there is a fpring
of water, which exactly refembles the
Pyrmont fpa, and whofe component
parts are nearly the fame. Mr. Wollafton drank the waters, and ufed the
baths for two months, and left Pifa in
much better health and fpirits than when
he entered it. This city, through the
middle of which flows the river Arno,
is large and well built, and its inhabitants
are polite to ftrangers. The markets are
well fupplied with all forts of provifions
and fruits, at the moft reafonable rate;
and houfe-rents are extremely cheap.

With

With regard to air, I fhould prefer it as a *winter* refidence to any part of Italy. But, were I called upon to point out a fummer refidence, my choice would fall upon Sienna, whofe fituation is lofty, and whofe air has a juft reputation for its falubrity.

From Pifa we went, by way of Leghorn and Genoa, to the city of Nice, which we entered on the 27th day of September, 1782.

Permit me, Gentlemen, to take a wider field in defcribing this place than I have done in fpeaking of others, between it and Naples, as *thofe* are vifited rather becaufe they either lie in the route, or contain an abundance of curiofities, than

becaufe

becaufe they are breathed upon by an air deemed fit to reftore a decaying con-ftitution, I have therefore avoided to enlarge on them, as making no part of my fubject: but as *this* place is fo much reforted to by Englifh invalids, and as it is my earneft wifh to render them all the information and affiftance in my power, I feel myfelf particularly called on to be more minute in my account of it.

The city of Nice is the capital of that county in Piedmont, which belongs to the King of Sardinia. This county is about eighty miles in length, by about thirty in breadth: it contains feveral towns and a great many villages, all of which, except the capital, are fituated amongft the mountains. The city itfelf is fituated in a plain, which is about five

miles

miles in length, by three in breadth, and is bounded on the weft by the river Var, which divides it from Provence, in the South of France; on the fouth, by the Mediterranean fea, which comes up to the walls; and on the north by the maritime Alps, which begin from the back of this plain, with hills of gentle afcent, rifing by degrees into lofty mountains, and forming a fweep or amphitheatre ending at Montalbano, which projects into the fea, and overhangs the town to the eaft. The river Paglion, which defcends from the mountains, and is fupplied only by the rains or the melting of the fnows, wafhes the walls of the city, and falls into the fea on the weft. The channel of this river is very wide, but never full of water, except after heavy rains or the melting of the

3   fnows

ſnows in the Alpine mountains, when it becomes a formidable torrent.

The country about Nice is moſt delightful and pleaſant, all which, from the Caſtle Hill, or even from the ramparts, is taken in at one view, and looks like an enchanted ſpot, or garden of Paradiſe; the whole plain being highly cultivated with vines, pomegranates, almonds, &c. as alſo with every ſpecies of evergreens, as oranges, lemons, citrons, and bergamots. The hills are ſhaded to the tops with olive trees, amongſt which are interſperſed the caſſinas, or country houſes, which add great warmth to the landſcape. The gardens belonging to them are full of roſe-trees, carnations, ranunculas, violets, and all ſorts of flowers,

flowers, which bloom the whole winter. Here indeed vegetation continues the whole year, and the inhabitants may juſtly be ſaid to enjoy a perpetual ſpring; for although nature repoſes herſelf during the winter months in moſt other countries, ſhe is ever active and indefatigable here.

As Mr. Wollaſton and myſelf were taking a ride, on the 22d of December, we ſaw the payſans, or farmers, gathering their olives on the hills, and in the vallies gathering their oranges and lemons, and mowing and making their hay; which they aſſured us they did four times in the year. The ſun in this climate, during the winter months, produces a heat nearly equal to that in the month of May in England. Such alſo is the ſere-

nity

nity of the air, that one fees nothing
above one's head, for months together,
but the moft charming blue expanfe without clouds.

The walks near this city are very
pleafant, and numerous; but the rides,
which are very much confined, are ftony
and difagreeable, except the two where
the carriages pafs; the one by the fea
fide, as far as the Var, about five miles;
and the other, about two miles from the
New Gate, on the Turin road, between
two lofty mountains, by the fide of the
river Paglian.

There is a market tolerably well fupplied with provifions, fuch as beef, pork,
mutton, and veal. The lamb is fmall,

D   and

and often poor; the poultry is very indifferent, and dear; but game is plen-
tiful, and reafonable, unlefs there be
much company. There is no fcarcity of
fifh; but the beft forts are dear; the
butter is good, and rather cheap, the
bread very indifferent indeed. The
greateft part of their provifions come
from Piedmont.

I hope I have given a juft account of
this beautiful little country, with refpect
to its external and pleafing form: let us
now look into its inconveniences, and
the more interefting parts with refpect to
thofe who come here for the purpofe of
recovering loft health. That moft ufeful
article in life, water, is generally drawn
from deep wells, and is fo very hard as
to

to be fit for few ufes. The only water in the city fit for drinking is that in the well of the convent of the Dominican Friars, in the Great Square, which, being expofed a fhort time to the air, becomes foft and good. Thefe friars are fo kind and civil, that they refufe no inhabitant, who afks their leave, and ufes it with moderation.

Amongft the many difagreeable things are to be reckoned the incredible number of flies, fleas, bugs, gnats, &c. Thefe never fink into a torpid ftate, as in colder climates, but are troublefome all the winter. Gnat-nets are fixed to all the beds, without which there would be no fleeping. The trades-people are extremely impofing in all their dealings;

D 2 and

and the Englifh in general, with every degree of circumfpection, cannot guard againft their knavery. Servants of every kind are the moft abandoned cheats, flovenly and lazy; the lodging-houfes exceffively dear, both in town and country, which they force you to take for fix months, or they will not fuffer you to enter. Care muft be taken to make the moft particular agreements upon every occafion; for if the leaft tittle be left to their honour or good-nature, you will pay dearly for falfely attributing to them qualities which this clafs of the inhabitants very rarely poffefs.

I truft, Gentlemen, that you will not confider the above remarks as *impertinent* to the fubject which I promifed to handle.

It

It is important to the cure that the patient fhould enjoy every comfort, and poffefs an equal and calm mind; for in as much as his quiet is difturbed, or his temper ruffled, by fo much is his cure retarded. It was not therefore improper to ftate the difficulties which every man muft here expect to encounter.

But the climate now demands our attention. Are thefe inconveniences fo overbalanced as to become light, when weighed with the benefits which infirm health may expect to receive from the purity of the air? Let us examine this queftion. The air, as I before obferved, is ferene, and perfectly free from moifture: whatever clouds may be formed by evaporation from the furrounding fea feldom

hover

hover long over this fmall territory, but
are attracted by the mountains, and
there fall in rain or fnow. As for thofe
which gather from more diftant quarters,
their progrefs hitherward is obftructed by
thefe very Alpine mountains, which
rife one over another to an extent of many
leagues.

The air being thus dry and elaftic,
it follows that it muft be agreeable to the
conftitutions of thofe who labour under
diforders arifing from weak nerves, obftructed perfpiration, relaxed fibres, a
vifcidity of lymph, and a languid circulation. But as the atmofphere is ftrongly
impregnated with marine falt, which is
eafily difcoverable when there are ftrong
breezes from the fea, the furface of the
hands

hands being covered with a falt brine very fenfible to the tafte, fcorbutic diforders are common amongft this people. This quality of the air arifes from the high mountains which hem it in, and prevent its free communication with the furrounding atmofphere, in which the faline particles. would be diffufed and foftened, were there a free circulation.

This country hath continually variable winds, as it is furrounded by mountains, capes, and ftraits. By thefe fharp and fudden variations the human conftitution is no lefs affected than by the current of air : whilft the fun gives fo great heat, that you can fcarce take any exercife out of doors, without being thrown into a breathing fweat; the wind is frequently fo keen and piercing, that it too often produces the

mif-

mifchievous effects of the pores thus fuddenly opened; as colds, pleurifies, peripneumonies, ardent fevers, rheumatifms, &c. The heat rarefies the blood and juices, while the cold wind conftringes the fibres, and obftructs perfpiration. Hence in the winter months you never meet an inhabitant of Nice without his cloak wrapped about him, and his mouth and nofe ftopped with his handkerchief or muff, that the air might not enter into his lungs without paffing through a medium to foften it. Hence alfo he wears feveral flannel waiftcoats and the warmeft cloathing.

I was refident in this city upwards of eight months, namely, from the 25th of September to the firft day of June

fol-

following. I obſerved that the moſt
cold and dangerous months are thoſe
about the time of the vernal equinox.
Great care ſhould then be taken to guard
againſt the diſeaſes ariſing from obſtructed
perſpiration ; for, although the ſun be
intenſely hot, the eaſt and north-eaſt
winds (which blow almoſt conſtantly
during the months of March, April, and
May) from paſſing over the Alps and
Apennine mountains, whoſe tops are
always covered with ſnow, become extremely ſharp and penetrating. This
intemperature ſometimes laſts (as was
the caſe that year) to the middle or end
of May, when the ſnow on the neareſt
mountains begins to melt, and the air
becomes more mild and balmy. But in
the progreſs of a few weeks, the heat is

E   ſo

fo difagreeable, that a more temperate climate ought to be fought for. An invalid would, in my opinion, act more prudently, if he left the city the firft week in March.

To what difeafes then are the inhabitants of this country moft fubject? They are troubled with fevers of various kinds, in moft or all of which I found the lungs concerned; fcrophulas, rheumatifms, opthalmias, fcorbutic putrid gums, with ulcers and eruptions of various forts. The moft prevailing diftemper feemed to be a marafmus. I frequented their hofpitals often, and found thefe to be the chief difeafes; all which are fimilar to thofe in the hofpitals of Naples and other towns near the fea coaft in Italy. But if the

the inhabitants themfelves, whofe very looks betray marks of ill health, afforded not fuch numerous proofs of the un-wholefomenefs of this air, I am, alas! furnifhed with too many by my unhappy countrymen, who wintered there in 1783. There were twenty-four families, befides feveral fingle Englifh gentlemen, the whole of which amounted to the number of 136 perfons; and I believe very few of thofe who came there on account of the air, found the expected benefit: I can except only two; one, an elderly gouty gentleman; the other, a tender, weakly, low-fpirited gentleman, with a flow fever at times; but *both* had found lungs. The only confumptive cafes I faw at Nice, were fix young gentlemen, and a lady rather advanced in years, all

E 2   of

of whom died in the courfe of the winter. Three of thefe young men were fo active and cheerful at times, even to a day before their deaths, that there was reafon to hope for their recovery. Had they ftaid in England, or fome parts of the South of France, I firmly believe that four of the fix, *if not now alive*, would at leaft have protracted their days. I attended a great many of the Englifh, who came to Nice in health, in violent inflammatory fevers, in all of which the lungs were concerned. Our own family was not without its fhare of the bad effects of this climate. Mr. Wollafton, in the courfe of our ftay there, had three very fevere attacks of inflammatory fevers, and left that place fo very ill, that I had very little hopes of his ever feeing England more.

Mrs.

Mrs. Wollaston had very violent inflammations in her eyes at various times, head-achs, and a fever which confined her for fome weeks. My wife, a remarkably healthy woman, was feized with an inflammatory fever, which obliged her to keep the chamber upwards of three months, and at length terminated in a large abfcefs in one of her arms, which faved her life. With refpect to myfelf, who have as good a conftitution as nature ever conferred on man, and have been a ftranger in general to all difeafes, I had not been there ten days before I was feized with violent head-achs and acute rheumatic pains, which perfecuted me, with very little intermiffion, during the whole time of our ftay. My eyes and teeth, although remarkably ftrong, were

affected

affected in fuch a manner, that there is
reafon to apprehend that a refidence of a
very few years in this place would de-
prive me of both.

In the courfe of the account which I
have given you of Nice and Naples, you
cannot but obferve, Gentlemen, that the
climate and difeafes of *both* are fimilar;
that the effects which *both* produced on
our own family were nearly the fame,
and that the air of *both* is demonftrated by
example to be too fharp and penetrating
for confumptive patients.   Remains there
then to be tried any plan which may be
preferable? I will fufpend my journey
for a while, and be hardy enough to
fuggeft one which appears to me to chal-
lenge fairer hopes of fuccefs.

The

The moderate warmth and refreshing verdure of England are surely preferable to the sultry suns and changeable piercing winds of Italy. Let the consumptive patient make choice of Abergavenny, in South Wales, for his summer residence; use proper exercise, and drink goats whey. If he be of a lax habit, the Tilbury waters will be an excellent common drink. As soon as winter threatens approach, let him remove to the environs of Bristol, take horse exercise on the Downs as often as the weather and his strength will admit, and drink the Hot-well waters, under the direction of an able physician, who will assist him likewise in the application of proper medicine and diet. Should this method prove ineffectual, I should advise

a trial

a trial of the South of France. The parts to which I fhould give the preference for a *winter* refidence, are the environs of the city of Avignon, near the famous fountain of Vauclufe, Nifmes, or Pezenas, where the air is as dry, and much more pure than that of Italy. Thefe places are well fupplied with provifions, and houfe-rents and lodgings are not unreafonable; circumftances not altogether undeferving the attention of thofe who are under the difagreeable neceffity of feeking health beyond the limits of their own country. But my chief reafon for preferring thefe places to all others in France, is its more diftant fituation from the fea, whofe influence I conceive to be obnoxious in thefe warm climates. As the fun, during the months of June, July, and

7

Auguft,

Auguſt, is extremely powerful in Provence and Languedoc, let him remove
to Berrage or Banniers, both ſituated
amongſt the mountains, where the air in
three months is temperate and agreeable,
the living cheap, good cow's and goat's
milk in plenty, and ſome of the waters
in each place beneficial in diſeaſes of the
lungs, as have been experienced by many
who have drunk them under thoſe complaints. The Cevennes mountains alſo,
which abound with many medicinal
ſprings, afford ſeveral places of an agreeable ſummer retreat. In November, let
him return to his winter's reſidence. If,
after a fair trial for two years, he ſhould
find no relief, I ſhould fear that his diſ-
order was beyond the reach of human
ſkill. Let me add another remark,

F   before

before I quit this topic. It is commonly
thought that the moist and foggy atmo-
sphere of Great Britain, so loaded as it
is with humid particles, renders the inhabitants more liable to catarrhs, rheu-
matisms, fevers, pulmonary complaints,
and other diseases arising from obstructed
perspiration, than those of milder climates; but let the inhabitants on the sea
coasts of Italy, who are so horribly afflicted with these diseases, and than whom
there are not more miserable objects in
all Europe, testify to the contrary of this
received idea.

But, to resume our journey.—Long
before our departure from Nice, I was
convinced that Mr. Wollaston had con-
cretions in the gall bladder, and biliary
ducts.

ducts. His stomach was so weak, that little food and few medicines would stay upon it. He was seldom free from pain, and was attacked every four or five weeks with most excruciating pains in the region of the liver, vomitings, with obstinate costivenefs, and white stools: Mr. Birbeck, the English conful, a most worthy and friendly man, advifed me by all means to take Mr. Wollafton, as foon as he was able, to the Hot Baths of Balaruc, in Languedoc, where, having been entirely cured himfelf of a palfy by the use of them, he had frequent opportunities of feeing their falutary effects on jaundices, which had refufed to yield to the moft powerful remedies.

As

As other means had failed, I determined to give thefe waters a trial, and accordingly we quitted Nice on the firft of June, 1783, having been there upwards of eight months. Aix, which lies in the route, has warm baths much of the fame nature with thofe of Buxton, in Derbyfhire. It is remarkable, that the cough and flow fever, which hung about my wife from the time of the fevere attack fhe fuftained at Nice, were quickly removed by drinking thefe waters and ufing thefe baths. They likewife agreed fo well with Mr. Wollafton, that in the fpace of a month he fo far recruited his ftrength as to be able to proceed on his journey. We went by eafy ftages to Avignon, Nifmes, and Montpellier, and reached Balaruc on the

twelfth

twelfth of July. This little town is about twenty miles from Montpellier, and two miles out of the great road to the city of Thouloufe. Thefe baths were very famous in the times of the Romans, which not only hiftory, but the many antiquities round them, and fome curious medals and ftatues lately difcovered there, clearly demonftrate.

On the fecond day after our arrival, Mr. Wollafton was taken with one of his fits as violently as ufual; but by the affiftance of the waters and baths they fubdued it in three days; whereas all his former fits, with every affiftance which medicine could give him, were of nine or ten days duration. He continued the ufe of them for a fortnight, accord-

according to the rules and cuftoms of the baths, at the end of which time his countenance, appetite, and ftrength, proclaimed a perfect cure. Mr. Wollafton, for the fpace of three months, drank the waters, and ufed the baths at intervals, although he was not abfolutely in want of them. With what pleafure do I inform you, Sir, that, fince that happy period, he has experienced no return of his fits, nor the fmalleft fymptom of a difeafed liver, notwithftanding the feverity of laft winter, than which, the inhabitants of Montpellier affured me, they never remembered one more cold or violent. But, however firmly eftablifhed might be the reftoration of Mr. Wollafton's health, I refolved to make another vifit to Balaruc this fpring: there was no ap-

parent

parent neceſſity for it: it may be an act of ſupererogation: but at all events it can do no harm, and may poſſibly bid defiance to a relapſe.

I have the honour, Sir, to addreſs this letter to you from the Baths, where it is our intention to ſtay a fortnight, and afterwards to ſet out on our journey for England. So numerous and ſurpriſing are the cures effected by theſe waters, that I think I cannot do my country a greater ſervice than by publiſhing the ingenious treatiſe on their medicinal virtues, written by Monſ. Pouzaire, the reſident phyſician. I ſhall order the original French to be printed, and with it a tranſlation into Engliſh, which I have made for the benefit of

thoſe

thole who are not masters of the French tongue. I shall also subjoin to it some account of the cures which have fallen under the testimony of my own eye.

As I am now resident in the wine countries, excuse me if I here digress, to make one general remark. In every part of Europe through which I have travelled, it has been my observation, that the peasants and common labourers, who have wine for their ordinary drink, are inferior both in size and strength to the English, Welch, Scotch, or Irish husbandmen, who drink nothing but milk, butter-milk, water, or even thin small beer. The longer I live, the more I am convinced that wine, and all other fermented liquors, are most pernicious

to

to the human conftitution ; and that for the prefervation of health, and exhilaration of fpirits, there is no drink equal or comparable to pure, fimple, good water. Let me not be deemed arrogant, if I venture to call myfelf a tolerable judge ; as it has been my common drink between thirty and forty years; and I believe there are few men living, who, at my age, are bleffed with better health and fpirits than myfelf.

Amongft the moft pleafing remembrances of my paft travels, there are none which give me more real fatisfaction than the profeffional fervices I had opportunity to render to great numbers of my difeafed countrymen, whom chance threw in my way in the various

G   parts

parts through which we paſſed. It ſur-
priſed me not a little to find how few of
them were provided with conveniences,
to *them* of an indiſpenſible neceſſity.
You well know, Sir, that a drug
of an inferior or bad quality is alone
ſufficient to aggravate the ſymptoms
it was intended to remove, and thus
ſubvert the well-founded expectations of
the ableſt phyſicians. As, therefore, but
few are to be had on the continent of
France and Italy, and thoſe few of the
moſt *ordinary* quality; let the invalid be
furniſhed with a cheſt well filled with
the beſt Engliſh medicines. He will
thus alſo guard againſt the ſhameful
charges of foreign apothecaries, whoſe
extortion is only to be equalled by their
ignorance. As I would at all times wiſh

to

to avoid the moft diftant appearance of perfonality, I feel myfelf reluctant to particularife any individual; but one apothecary there is at Nice, whofe conduct is fo notorious, that thofe of my countrymen who have already employed him will, I am perfuaded, hold me juftifiable in requefting that others may be advifed to avoid him. His drugs are bad, his advice worfe, and his infolence infupportable. His impofing charges far outdo the impofitions of his unconfcionable brethren. He calls himfelf the Englifh apothecary, only becaufe he fpeaks a little broken Englifh, and by various arts procures recommendations to moft of the Englifh families who come there.—Behold here the portrait of Monfieur F——! The only apothe-

cary

cary I there found with tolerable medicines, or in any degree acquainted with
his bufinefs, is a Mr. Paffaro, who lives
in the ftreet leading to the Jews quarter.

The patient would do well alfo (if it
be in his power) to take with him an
Englifh phyfician, as the foreign phy-
ficians, but particularly thofe of Italy,
are little competent to undertake the
cure of thofe acute difeafes, which fo
often arife in thofe warm climates.
Their manner of treatment is totally
different from the methods adopted in
England. Bleedings, glyfters, and bou-
illons, are their panaceas; nor does it
ever occur to them that nature may
receive as it were new life by a timely
and well-applied method of practice.

When

When the dreadful train of evils which follow the ufe of unclean and damp fheets be maturely confidered, it cannot be thought an improper caution to advife the patient to carry with him his own bed linen.

Thus equipped let him fet out on his foreign expedition. But let me be pardoned, if I hazard one prediction. Soon will he regret the temperate climate which he had forfaken for the fultry funs and variable winds of more fouthern regions—deeply will he lament, in cafe of an unforefeen and dangerous attack, that, to the advice of his travelling phyfician, he cannot join the fuperior fkill of Sir George Baker

BAKER—and dearly, too dearly, will he learn to fet a proper value on the bleffings of his native country, which excel all others beyond compare.

I am,

SIR,

With the greateft refpect and efteem,

Your obedient, humble Servant,

BENJAMIN PUGH.